NOV 2004

You need feel embarrassed no longer. Here, in simple words and fantastically complicated pictures, is the fearlessly outspoken exposé that rips the lid off the pressing problems of our times, namely:

1. Who is stronger, Captain Marbles or Superduperman?

2. What shocking new evidence lies behind the charge that newspapers are the real cause of adult delinquency?

3. Can the Army-McCarthy show be revived as a TV panel quiz?

4. What is Roger Price's *Vital Message?*

Answers to these and other important questions can be found inside. More precious than rubies, more stimulating than Nembutal, The MAD Reader is a book you will want to read and treasure as a keepsake. Afterwards it can be used for wrapping fish.

THE M

ibooks
new york
www.ibooksinc.com

DISTRIBUTED BY
SIMON & SCHUSTER, INC

REA

written by..**HARVEY KURTZMA**

drawn by...**JACK DAVIS**
BILL ELDER
WALLACE WOOD

AD

DER

with a
Vital Message
from
ROGER PRICE

GOOD
LORD!

ibooks, inc.
24 West 25th Street
New York, NY 10010

The ibooks World Wide Web Site Address is:
http://www.ibooksinc.com

Visit www.madmag.com

ISBN 0-7434-3491-9
First ibooks, inc. printing March 2002
10 9 8 7 6 5

Printed in the U.S.A.

CONTENTS

A MESSAGE FROM
THE PUBLISHER

A friend asked me the other day what books changed my life. I paused for a moment and said, "Other than the Bible?" He nodded. I thought.

"The *MAD* paperbacks by Harvey Kurtzman and the stories of Ray Bradbury," I replied.

This particular friend was in his late twenties and knew of neither. I knew that I could refer him to the *Collected Stories of Ray Bradbury* for the seminal works of the American fantasy writer, but as for Kurtzman's *MAD* paperbacks, they were out of print, having sold millions of copies from the '50s to the '80s before dropping out of sight.

Kurtzman and Bradbury were astral twins in a way. Both were popularized by E.C. Comics (one authorized, one not so authorized). Both were brought to new audiences by the groundbreaking team of Ian and Betty Ballantine, the revolutionary publishers of Ballantine Books. Bradbury's *Fahrenheit 451* was published in a limited asbestos edition by Ballantine; Kurtzman's *The MAD Reader* was the first paperback collection ever of a comic book. Bradbury's *The Martian Chronicles* will forever be viewed as classic of the '50s; Kurtzman's *MAD* will forever define satire for the Eisenhower era.

I am fortunate to have been friends with both Ray and Harvey. They were friendly with each other through a bond formed annually at many San Diego comic book conventions. They also shared a deep passion for the classic comic strips of the '30s and '40s, which provide the fodder for many of the stories in this collection.

Harvey was a remarkable man—generous with his time, gentle with his family and friends, and enamored of his craft. He drew the most pleasure in gathering together all of the cartoonists he knew in a big party each year catered by his equally witty wife, Adele.

As you read this book, whether as a trip down memory lane or as your first encounter with the genius of Kurtzman, Wood, Elder, Davis from that "Usual Gang of Idiots," please savor every detail-packed panel. Each was rendered lovingly by men who loved the comics they wrote and drew, often suffering for their craft.

After 50 years, their *MAD Reader* is as fresh as ever.

—Byron Preiss

INTRODUCTION
by Grant Geissman

The book you are now reading is a facsimile reprint of *The MAD Reader*, and is the first in a new series of reprints (published by ibooks) of the early *MAD* paperbacks.

The original version of *The MAD Reader* (published in December 1954 by Ballantine Books) was actually a first on several fronts. It was the first of what would later become a long line of over 200 paperbacks featuring reprints of material from *MAD*. And it was the first paperback to feature material that was originally published in comic books.

For the uninitiated, *MAD* began life in October 1952 as a 10¢, full-color comic, and was one of the books published by William M. Gaines's E.C. comic book line (including such titles as *Tales from the Crypt*, *The Vault of Horror*, and *Weird Science*.) Gaines also published two war comics, *Two-Fisted Tales* and *Frontline Combat*, which were written and edited by a young man named Harvey Kurtzman, who also illustrated a fair number of the stories and covers for these books. Kurtzman was a meticulous worker who strove to invest his war stories with realism and human drama. He felt that he couldn't write a story until it was thoroughly researched, a process that included reading actual war accounts and talking with veterans. Needles to say, this laborious process could—and very often did—take weeks. In the comics game, speed was the most valuable commodity, followed by talent, because virtually all artists and writers were paid by the job. The more material they could crank out, the more they would earn. Although Kurtzman was doing some of the finest work ever done in comics—then or now—he was simply having trouble making ends meet. He appealed to Gaines for a raise, but Gaines was in a conundrum. Although he sympathized with Kurtzman's request, he paid his freelancers by the job and, in editor Kurtzman's case, by the book. And although Gaines loved what Kurtzman did, his two war comics sold only marginally well compared with E.C.'s flagship horror titles like *Tales from the Crypt* and *The Haunt of Fear* (which were written and edited by another writer/artist/editor named Al Feldstein). Feldstein was handling seven titles to Kurtzman's two, and bringing in the lion's share of the company revenues besides. Gaines's publishing philosophy was somewhat unusual: he didn't care what each individual title brought in as long as the overall revenues for the company were healthy. Still, he couldn't quite reconcile Kurtzman's request for a raise. The solution: If Harvey could do one additional comic book title for E.C., something that would be easy and that didn't require all the tedious research, his income would increase by 50 percent.

Accounts vary as to who actually proposed the new comic book as a humor title. Gaines always said that it was his suggestion, because the first material of Kurtzman's that he ever saw (and that caused him to hire Kurtzman in the first place) were the humorously oddball

Hey Look! pages that he had done for Stan Lee's Timely Comics. Kurtzman, on the other hand, says it was his brainchild, because humor was something he had done before and loved doing. In the end, it matters not, because *MAD* was Kurtzman's baby all the way. With his usual attention to detail, Kurtzman wrote virtually everything that appeared in the *MAD* comic book, and designed and/or illustrated all of its covers. He also provided tissue paper layouts of each story for the artists to follow; to go substantially off Kurtzman's vision was some-thing the artists were routine-ly instructed *not* to do. Within the framework of these layouts, however, the artists were encouraged to contribute freely, especially if it took the form of added sight gags or other marginal *MAD*-ness.

Art credit unavailable (late 1960s)

The first few issues of the fledgling title actually lost money, but Gaines (again unlike other comic book publishers of the time) was game to let the book ride and see if it could find its audi-ence. By the fifth issue, *MAD* had taken off, and within a very short time they were printing upward of a million copies of each issue, and selling 86 percent of its print run—a staggering percentage.

The little *MAD* comic book had become a bona-fide phenomenon and was wildly popular on college campuses, reaching an older age demographic (unusual for a comic book). After *MAD* had been publishing for about two years, innovative paperback publisher Ian Ballantine came to E.C. with the idea of doing a paperback collection of reprints from *MAD*. Kurtzman and Ballantine editor Bernard Shir-Cliff handpicked the book's contents. Kurtzman also designed the cover, which is noteworthy for being the first time the face of the "What—Me Worry?" kid, later christened "Alfred E. Neuman" by *MAD*, appeared prominently on the cover of a *MAD* publication. Kurtzman had seen the face on a postcard tacked to his editor's wall at Ballantine, and had immediately decided that it had a suitably vapid expression. The foreword ("A Vital Message")

Art by Robert Grossman (1975)

was contributed by Roger Price, who was then having great success with his *Droodles* syndicated comic strip and with a series of best-selling *Droodles* books. (Not so coincidentally, Price also had some books that were also published by Ballantine.)

The *MAD Reader* was an instant hit, prompting Ballantine to go back to press with it a surprising number of times: it went through six printings between December 1954 and December 1955. The book (and the four other subsequent volumes released by Ballantine) remained continuously in print for nearly twenty years. Three different times during that twenty-year history, Ballantine trotted out

new sets of distinctly varied cover art, including a "pop art" version, a set of airbrush/stylized covers by Robert Grossman (which Bill Gaines hated) and a latter-day set of covers by beloved *MAD* cover artist Norman Mingo. Thus, fans coming upon the series at various points in its publishing history would be relating to very different sets of cover images.

Leading off *The MAD Reader* is "Superduperman!" (*MAD* #4, April-May 1953, masterfully illustrated by Wallace Wood), a biting satire

Art by Norman Mingo (1976)

of the then-ongoing lawsuit between DC Comics, which published *Superman*, and Fawcett, which published the competing *Captain Marvel*. DC claimed that *Captain Marvel* was too close to *Superman* for comfort, and waged a vitriolic—not to mention expensive—lawsuit against Fawcett that dragged on for years. The suit might have gone on practically forever, until Fawcett, noticing declining sales on super hero comic books, decided the suit wasn't worth fighting any longer and threw in the towel, suspending publication of all of its comic book titles. Meanwhile, the suits at DC were not at all amused by "Superduperman!," and they threatened *MAD* publisher Bill Gaines with legal action. This prompted Gaines to promise not to do it again, a promise he would eventually break quite a few times over the course of *MAD*'s long publishing history.

"Newspaper!" (*MAD* #16, October 1954, illustrated by Jack Davis) is Kurtzman's reverse play on the "comic books are ruining our children" sentiment that was being loudly voiced by the guardians of morality at the time. Another Davis piece, "Do People Laugh at You for Reading Comics?" (*MAD* #12, June 1954), is actually a reformatted page that originally appeared as a "house" ad for subscriptions to the *MAD* comic book. (It should be noted that all of the material appearing in this book was rearranged from its original vertical comic book layouts to accommodate the horizontal—and sideways!—layouts required by the paperback format.)

Another American institution, the "typical teenage" comic book *Archie*, is given the Kurtzman treatment in "Starchie" (*MAD* #12, June 1954, illustrated by Bill Elder). Turning such "goodie-goodie" characters on their head was a concept Kurtzman would return to again and again, both in *MAD* and in his later work for other publishers. Elder's zany artwork (and the extra gags written on the walls, appearing in the background, and just about anywhere else he could find a spot) set much of the tone for the early *MAD* comics. As Kurtzman told comic historian John Benson, "I think Will's 'chicken-fat' humor was very necessary to the feeling that *MAD* generated. As a matter of fact, Will did much to set the cartoon approach that was used for years in *MAD*—the detail, the asides."

Elder's other contributions to *The MAD Reader* are "Dragged Net!" (*MAD* #11, May 1954) and "Gasoline Valley!" (*MAD* #15, September 1954). "Dragged Net!" lampoons *Dragnet*, Jack Webb's hit television vehicle, which he wrote, directed, and starred in. *Dragnet* had begun on radio on 1949 and had made a very successful transition to the small screen in January 1952, finishing as the fourth most popular show of the 1952 fall season. The show ran on NBC until 1959, and enjoyed a revival on NBC from 1967-1970. Here Elder's "chicken-fat" style is readily apparent, with numerous sight gags and the insertion throughout the story of a caricature of Elder's own Yiddish mother ("Villie? Villie Elder?"). Also noteworthy is Kurtzman's reiteration of composer Walter Schumann's classic "Dragnet March" ("DOMM DA DOM DOMM").

"Gasoline Valley!" is Kurtzman's take on Frank King's popular and long-running *Gasoline Alley* syndicated strip, a strip that was as wholesomely Americana as apple pie. It was also the only comic strip of its time—or any time, for that matter—in which the main characters actually aged. Elder here is a master craftsman, producing a dead-on carbon copy of King's clean, somewhat sedate drawing style.

Wallace Wood was the obvious choice to illustrate "Flesh Garden!" (*MAD* #11, May 1954), which parodies Alex Raymond's *Flash Gordon* newspaper comic strip. Wood was greatly influenced by Raymond and here clearly savors the opportunity to pay a satirical tribute to one of his idols. Wood's "Flesh Garden" bears a strong resemblance to Buster Crabbe, who played Flash in the *Flash Gordon* movie serials. Wood's women, rendered almost fifty years ago, are still sexy and titillating and made a lasting impression on *MAD*'s readers in the button-down Fifties.

"What's My Shine!" (illustrated by Jack Davis, *MAD* #17, November 1954) juxtaposes the venerable TV quiz show *What's My Line?* with the notorious Senator Joseph McCarthy/Army hearings. The politically ambitious senator headed a subcommittee that was investigating the alleged presence of Communists in the U.S. Army. These widely televised (and obsessively watched) hearings, in which McCarthy's "Red scare" tactics were ultimately shown to be little more than what was then described as "reckless cruelty," ruined the Wisconsin senator's political career. As Kurtzman told John Benson, "I never thought of myself as political. McCarthy was a special case; he seemed to be so dangerous. So I did something that I don't normally do: I politicized a feature. But when McCarthy came along, he was so obvious. And so evil. It was like doing a satire on Hitler. Very easy to do." After McCarthy's death in 1960, "What's My Shine!" was dropped from future printings of *The MAD Reader*, replaced by "The Face Upon the Floor!" and the

"Armstronger Tire" ad parody ("Armstrong Tires Grip the Road" is the specific ad slogan Kurtzman is parodying here).

"The Face Upon the Floor!" (*MAD* #10, March-April 1954, illustrated by Jack Davis) was actually a visual realization of the classic poem by H. Antoine D'Arcy. This was one of several classic poems that got a similar treatment in *MAD*'s early comic book issues. Worth special mention is the last panel, which was rendered by the inimitable Basil Wolverton, at Harvey Kurtzman's request. A proponent of the "spaghetti and meatball" school of illustration, Wolverton's ropy-looking artwork fit well in *MAD*. While this was Wolverton's first work for the publication, it wasn't his last: he did several more specialty pieces for both the comic book and the magazine incarnations of *MAD*.

Jack Davis gets the closing spot in this volume with "Lone Stranger!," which lampoons *The Lone Ranger* (*MAD* #3, February-March 1953). This article is most notable in that it was the first direct parody of a TV show to appear in *MAD*. *The Lone Ranger* had a phenomenally long run that straddled two show business mediums: it began on radio in 1933 and made the jump to the television screen in 1949. It soon became one of NBC's early television success stories, running until 1957. The program starred Clayton Moore as the Lone Ranger and Jay Silverheels as the faithful sidekick Tonto (parodied here as "Pronto"). The show's catchphrases, including "Who was that masked man?" and "Hi Ho Silver, away!," are suitably skewered here as well by Kurtzman's pen.

Serving as the final coda to the book is "The Men Who Make *MAD*," which consists of short humorous biographies of Kurtzman, Elder, Davis, and Wood. In all likelihood, these bios were also written by Harvey Kurtzman, specifically for use in *The MAD Reader*. Like "What's My Shine!," this page was eventually dropped from the many later printings of *The MAD Reader*.

Some of you (you know who you are) may be wondering why *anyone* would want to do a nice, high-quality facsimile reprint of material that is 50 years old. Happily, the answer lies ahead. Read on! HOOHAH!!

Grant Geissman *is the author of* Collectibly MAD, *(Kitchen Sink Press, 1995), and co-author with Fred von Bernewitz of* Tales of Terror! The EC Companion *(Gemstone/Fantagraphics, 2000). He compiled and annotated the "best of" volumes* MAD About the Fifties *(Little, Brown, 1997),* MAD About the Sixties *(Little, Brown, 1995),* MAD About the Seventies *(Little, Brown, 1996), and* MAD About the Eighties *(Rutledge Hill Press, 1999). He compiled and wrote liner notes for* MAD Grooves *(Rhino, 1996), and also contributed the introduction to* Spy vs. Spy: The Complete Casebook *(Watson-Guptill, 2001). When not reading MAD, Geissman is a busy Hollywood studio guitarist, composer, and "contemporary jazz" recording artist with 11 highly regarded albums released under his own name.*

A VITAL MESSAGE

By Roger Price

As you know (you probably don't but this is a clever psychological trick I use to get you on my side),

Atomic mutations the splitting of an atom releases powerful short-wave radiations which can alter genes and chromosomes in animals and plants and produce unusual off-spring or mutations.

MAD is a Literary Mutation caused by the radiations which result from the splitting of personalities.

Science has been forging ahead (against my advice) and has finally created a situation in which personality fission occurs as readily as french fried onions. If you don't think french fried onions occur readily then you don't understand nuclear psionics. Or my digestive system.

Gaines vs. Muslin Nevertheless, all of us are constantly being bombarded by tiny particles of misplaced schizophrenia (Sk–235), and nowhere is this type of radioactivity more plentiful than in the Entertaining Comics Factory. The emanations from the publisher, Bill Gaines, alone can bleach muslin at a distance of 25 feet (an accomplishment which he uses to pick up a couple of extra bucks on Saturdays). So it was, of course, inevitable that deep in the dank, chill, morbid (but cheerful) EC offices certain genes would be affected. They were. And after a lackluster period of gestation, MAD was born.

This doesn't mean that MAD is a freak. It's a natural product of selective evolution. And a necessary evolvement because it brings true creativity and dignity to a new medium of communication—the Comic Book. Many

Dignity yet Wrong Thinkers look upon the Comic Book as a substitute for Good Reading—whatever that is. Not so. The Comic Book offers a format to the writer-artist that is unique and will eventually take its place as a legitimate art form with the novel, television, films, and phenobarbitol. True, there are effects you can get in a novel that you can't get in a Comic Book. But there are points that can only be made in a Comic Book. For instance, the DRAGGED NET piece in this volume couldn't possibly be done as a dramatic sketch with actors. Neither could it be told in prose. It is an example of pure MAD.

As you may have gathered, I like MAD. There are several reasons why:

(1) It only costs ten cents.

(2) It's the first successful humor magazine to be started in this country since *The New Yorker*. The magazine business is generally in a stagnant or furshlugginer state. It's permeated with polls, pre-testing apparatus and the Idea that people must be given "what they want." This is nonsense which at best can only lead to their holding on (precariously) to the audience they already have. People want something new. They will buy a magazine that sounds like it knows something. MAD sounds like it knows something. I only wish I could figure what.

(3) MAD isn't satisfied to repeat its own successful formulas. It keeps experimenting, looking for original ways to utilize the Comic Book format.

(4) It costs a mere dime. (This volume of course is well worth the 35c whoever you borrowed it from paid for it as it contains the best from seven issues of MAD).

(5) MAD achieves what on the surface would seem to be impossible. It's even sillier than the things it lampoons. It takes broad, sometimes crude—but never vicious—swings at aspects of our culture that are foolish, sentimental, venal, stuffy or just plain corny. In other words it Gilds the Lily, it carries Carbohydrates to Farouk.

(6) Because of the sound-absorbing qualities of the paper, back issues of MAD are handy for putting under my POTRZE-BIE to deaden the hum. *Potrzebie hum*

(7) It has Style. This is because everything in MAD filters through the tiny but hyper-active brain of Harvey Kurtzman.

About two years ago Bill Gaines got the sensational idea

of doing a Comic Book that was actually comic. At the time, everyone but Harvey thought it was too revolutionary. So Gaines bombarded him with radiations from both his personalities and talked him into becoming the Editor. This means that Harvey writes all the pieces, does rough layouts for the drawings and avoids collusion as much as possible. His work is then abetted by the excellent and humorous art-work of Jack Davis, Bill *Special* Elder and Wallace Wood. Harvey was born *free offer* in 1924 and has been in Comics since he was sixteen. He is 5 feet 6 inches tall and has a physique that is just barely noticeable and a long expression. In fact—Harvey looks like a Beagle who is too polite to mention that someone is standing on his tail. This Beagleishness has certain compensations—he is never ordered off the grass in Central Park and Pretty Girls frequently stop on the street to scratch him behind the ears. Like many humorists, Harvey is a moralist and smiles rarely and with great effort. His ambition is to have everyone in the country subscribe to MAD.

MAD makes people laugh and this is a Good Thing. Because as someone once said (I can't remember whether it was Pliny the Elder or Virginia Mayo):

Vital *"Laughter is the great equalizer and*
message *soothes the baser passions and keeps people*
from fighting and quarreling and aids in
the digestive processes and in general is better than getting
hit by a taxi." Think it over. On second thought, read the representative pieces from MAD contained in this volume. Then, if you're still able to think, you can think it over. Good luck.

The MAD Reader

Faster than a speeding bullet! . . . *Ka-Pweeng!* More powerful than a locomotive! . . . *Chugachugachugachug!* Able to leap tall buildings in a single bound! . . . *Boinngswoosh!* . . . Look! Up in the sky! . . . It's a bird! . . . IT'S A PLANE! . . . IT'S . . . .

SUPERDUPERMAN!

FOR THIS IS THE ASSISTANT TO THE COPY BOY... CLARK BENT, WHO IS IN REALITY, *SUPERDUPERMAN!*

AN INCREDIBLY MISERABLE AND EMACIATED LOOKING FIGURE SHUFFLES FROM SPITOON TO SPITOON!

OUR STORY BEGINS HIGH UP IN THE OFFICES OF THAT FIGHTING NEWSPAPER,, 'THE DAILY DIRT'!

6

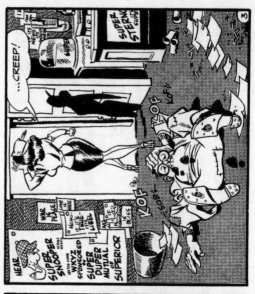

Insira a contagem aqui

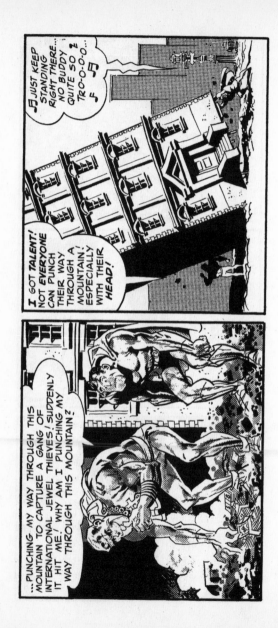

UP IN THE FIGHTING NEWSPAPER OFFICE OF THE 'DAILY DIRT'... GOING FROM SPITOON TO SPITOON...

...SHUFFLES AN INCREDIBLY WRETCHED AND MISERABLE LOOKING CREEP... CLARK BENT, ASSISTANT COPY BOY.

WHO IS IN REALITY, SUPERDUPERMAN! SO WHAT DOES IT ALL PROVE? IT PROVES *ONCE A CREEP, ALWAYS A CREEP!*

Youth! Even as we speak, grown-ups of America battle tirelessly to destroy evil reading matter that is corrupting youth! . . . However, behind their backs looms unchallenged evil reading matter that is corrupting Grown-ups! . . . Youth! . . . Save our Grown-ups! . . . SAVE THEM FROM THE BAD INFLUENCES OF . . . . .

NEWSPAPERS!

...like forinstance page 1!
With all kinds important
things going on in politics
here's what they put on page 1!

★★★★★ LATE LATE LATE LATE

DAILY POOP

PICTURE NEWSPAPER...PLENTY PICTURES

4¢ A POUND

Someday, October, 1954★ | 4¢ IN CITY LIMITS | 5¢ OUTSIDE COUNTRY LIMITS | 6¢ OUTSIDE EARTH LIMITS

MAN CARVES UP HIS GIRL FRIEND

Story on Page 4

Son of Skunk Farmer Weds Heiress

Story on Page 4

(POOP foto by Jack Davis)

Big Bloody Riot Boy! What violence there was on the docks yesterday. Note in Foreground above, [↑] policeman's teeth being smashed in by brass knuckles. Note in background, man, being clubbed on head with lead pipe, pushes thumb under other man's eye. Note plenty other bloody things by looking at photo closely.

(POOP foto by Jack Davis)

Girl Beaten Vava Voom s h o w s where she was bruised [→] when burglers broke into her apt. house. Although it was a neighbor's apt. they broke into; Vava was bruised while taking a shower.

Killer Admits Using Meat Grinder

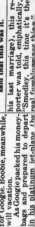

(POOP foto by Jack Davis)

...you skip page 2 and 3, which merely have to the ...important news...page 4! the best part...page 4!

Googie Divorces Zazie for Boobie

By Smedley Dirtdigger
DAILY POOP News Bureau

Yesterday, the most earth-shaking event in the history of our times took place when Googie Smidley, after a quick divorce from the Baroness Zazee Ley Smed, got secretly married to Boobie Van Smoodley at a modest little ceremony at the Taj Mahal.

After the wedding, a modest little reception was held at the Hollywood Bowl. The happy couple had this to say when quizzed by this reporter. "This time, Smedley, it's for keeps. This romance is the real thing and this time this is IT and for keeps this time and it's the real thing." This was Boobie's 12th marriage and Googie's 27th.

While Boobie is the wealthy heiress to the Van Smoodley Timber, Steel and Uranium fortune, Googie is the son of an illiterate, filthy, peasant skunk-farmer.

As to their future plans, Googie said that the honeymoon would have to be delayed since there are matters of grave concern and import to attend to ... matters that cannot wait. Like for instance, the construction of a special polomallet being hand-fashioned for Googie. Boobie, meanwhile, will vacation.

his last marriage], this reporter was told, emphatically, this time it's the ... in his platinum jet-plane. "I'm ... "They forb, grocer this."

Googie and Boobie as they said that this was it.

(POOP foto by J. Davis)

Full Details on Most Nauseating Crime Ever

Today, Sturdley Hockblock publicly confessed to the mostest sickeningest crime ever, in this city of Smerdley, and we have all the details down to the last gruesome little details.

Very Important People Arrive on Boat

(PROOF foto by Jack Davis)

The most importantest people ever, arrived on the S.S. Sturdley today. Above is Miss Baha Bam waving hello from rail of ship. Not that Miss Baha Bam had anything to do with arrivals . . . she was just passing by docks at time.

Googie With Foofoo While Boobie Vacations

By Dirtley Smedigger

The Bahamas—The most drooly incident ever witnessed by civilization took place this morning when Googie Smidley landed here on his own private platinum landing strip (by his eleventh marriage), for a rendezvous with Foofoo Smedd Lee.

Meanwhile, Boobie said she and Googie could not make a go of married life and she was instituting a divorce. Foofoo Smed Lee, wealthy heiress to Smed Lee Gold and Diamond fortune, announced modest little wedding, only 10,000 close friends to attend. When queried, Googie said, "Dirtley, this time it is positively IT," as he left, in his platinum diesel train.

Police Chief Smudley Smedley of Smerdley had this to say:

"Echhh!"

The body was discovered yesterday by 172 witnesses all over the city. This was because the body was in 172 packages all over the city. But you ain't heard nothing yet.

Hockblock was immediately apprehended through the efficiency of a mammoth police dragnet, a diligent manhunt by the organized citizenry, an announcement on "Gangbusters," and mainly, Hockblock gave himself up.

But now we come to main enjoyable part where Hockblock describes in detail how he committed murder like for instance what kind of butcher's cleaver he used, what type blood the victim had, what color blood, with closeups of the blood and like that.

Now all the teeny details the way Hockblock went about the murder was his victim. First he grabbed his victim and then he

(continued on pg. 780)

Googie is Mine Says Selma

By D. Irt

Selma Strudley, this evening, confirmed the devastating rumor that she and Googie Smidley will soon be married. Meanwhile, Foofoo Smedd Lee told reporters that her romance with Googie, after a long period of incessant bickering, has gone on the rocks.

Foofoo is the wealthy heiress to several large countries all over the world, and as she stood hand in hand with Googie at the entrance to Foofoo's modest little city, Googie informed this reporter that this was it! Outside, on Foofoo's private lake, on the deck of her private flattop, Googie's platinum jet Constellation was warming up for a business trip.

(PROOF foto by Jack Davis)

Googie: It's it. Googie and Foofoo tell world that this is it.

War Breaks Out in Far East. Millions Flee for Lives

It was heard today that the beginnings of a war have started in the far east. In the opinion of a leading advisor in this country, this war is so tightly linked to our strategic position in the world that it will undoubtedly lead this country and the rest of the world into war and it is diffi-cult to foresee how it will be possible to avoid using the atom and hydrogen bombs. A board of experts in an emer-gency round-table discussion agreed unanimously that this event in the far-east is defin-itely the beginning of the end of civilization.

False T...

...after that comes pages - like this with teenchy pieces of news stuck in edges!

OVERWEIGHT

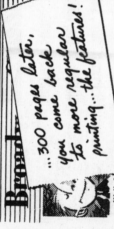

...300 pages later, you come back to more regular printing...the features!

Well, f... you today. I...er has plenty of dirt culled from Broadway f... some mighty interesting items down along that glamorous avenue of theatres, clubs, and the neon night-life. And here are some of the items, some of the dirt that this Broadway reporter picked up. Some of the items and dirt were: a hardly smoked cigar butt, a indian penny, a comic book with cover torn off, ½ pound silver paper from cigarette packages, 10 Planter's Peanuts wrappers I can send away for free stamps.

AND NOW, around the nightclubs with Smurdley Yeldrums: At the Stark Club I saw Zaza Zam chatting in a very chummy manner with producer, Sam Urdley. At the Twentyhousand Four Eight Club, Ludamey Zam, husband of the beauteous Zaza Zam, was seen sitting alone and this reporter chatted with him for a moment. At the Mocobombo, Sam Urdley, producer, was seen being punched in the nose while chatting with Ludamey Zam. At the Coq Roach, Zaza Zam seen also punched in the nose while chatting with Ludamey Zam. At the Chez Pigalle, this reporter seen punched in the nose by Zaza Zam.

WHAT ACTRESS?

AND NOW, the hottest item of the week: What T.V. actress has been frequently seen with what international playboy at what restaurant at what...

The Kwestioning Kameraman

By MURDLEY S.

THE POOP will pay $10 for every intelligent, thoughtful, important question submitted and used by this column.

QUESTION

...you ever get punched inna nose?

LOCATION

Down in the subway in various locations...on the platforms, in the trains, and on the tracks.

ANSWERS

Punchy Knucklehead, sandwich sign carrier: Nobody eva punched me. I don't give 'em the chanc't. I punch 'em fuyst. When guys pass me an' I don' like 'eir looks PUNCH! I let 'em have it.

Head knuckle Punched, process server: Yes, people always punch me in the nose. My job makes people mad. Sometimes people punch me for no reason. The other day some sad-wich-sign...

POOP PEOPLE'S LETTERS

Please give name and address and name of your lawyer with your letter

SHOOT

This city is going to the | GUSTED," and I want to voice my disagreement to this say? What will his agent have to say and what will his company do about what? In fact, what do all these goings on mean in the first place? If you know what, let me know what because I'd like to know myself

AND NOW, an open letter to Bopley Smurd: Dear Bopley, I am sending you this open letter because of the recent encounter you had with your public the other night when you got angry at your fans and refused to sign their autograph books. I am writing you this FAN open letter to remind you that it was the fans who put you where you are today. It was the fans who gave you your first break as a singer. Remember? It was the electrician and you were fixing the electric fans at the Stark Club and the night club owners heard you singing while you were fixing those electric fans? Remember? Hah, your bum, was member? That was your first break. I am writing you this letter just to remind you what those fans did for you. So last night, when your kicking screaming fans tore the sleeve from your coat, the leg from your pant, the hair from your head, there was no reason to get mad...no reason to start to strangle that little girl. She just wanted your socks for a souvenir. And mainly I am writing this open letter...I am writing you this open letter...because a closed letter would cost three cents postage and it's cheaper this way.

AND NOW, goings on about town. Pat Mike is about to sue Sam Tom! A.B. will double-cross C.D. in the morning! and E.F. is going to punch G.H. in the nose tomorrow! L.S. signed that contract with M.F.T. and it's rumored that Q.X. will O.K. that deal with O.K. How-

SILVER PAPER

ever, although Q.X. will O.K. that deal with O.K. Does Q.X. think O.K. is O.K.? If so, how can Q.X. O.K. if O.K. is not O.K.. that is, if O.K. is Q.X. and not O.K.. I mean O.K. rather then O.K.. er, the first O.K. rather then O.K as used the second time   Shall we get on to the next item!

AND NOW, this is your Broadway Gunk reporter, Smurdley Yeldrums closing with the final statement of wisdom that I pass along to you out there in order to give you something to think about today   and that final wise word is .. anybody want to buy silver-paper? I have ½ a pound which I will sell cheap.

zebie
Maybe One day, I went to the top of the Statue of Liberty and was accosted there by a thief who gave me a punch in the belly We were standing in the Statue of Liberty's nose, so although I was punched in the belly, I was punched in the nose.

Headpunch Knuckle, malcontented washdish washer: Has one the right to be punched in the nose in the core of this question. Don't let "big, interests" talk you into not getting punched in the nose. I hope that answers your question. Bobo Bom, stenographer. Quit following me or I'll give YOU a punch inna nose!

gradually, it is going to be dogs. There is a small band of dirty no-good self-seeking money-hungry political bums who alone are responsible for letting the city go to the dogs. And there is only one thing left to stop these dirty bunch of no good bums from letting this city go to the dogs. I say we must take them out and shoot them like dogs   take out all the dogs   every single dog..   and shoot them like dogs. That way, this city cannot go to the dogs. GREATLY DISGUSTED

GRIND UP
Your newspaper is the worst rag on the market. It is the most terrible bunch of junk I have ever seen. It isn't even fit to grind up and make into other paper again. It isn't even fit for thinking of grinding up and making into other paper It isn't even fit for making into paper for thinking of grinding up and making into other paper. I'll bet you don't print this. REALLY DISGUSTED

CRUMS
What a bunch of crums you are. I'll bet you don't print this. MUCH DISGUSTED

BUMS
Bums! I'll bet you don't print this. PLENTY DISGUSTED

I'LL
I'll bet you don't print this. GOOD AND DISGUSTED

STUPID
I read the letter yesterday by reader, "MOST DIS-

MOST DISGUSTED, then like you are the fundamental trouble with our whole social and political ideology. In other words, in answer to your statement "Women are stupid!" I say, men are stupid! DISGUSTED GIRL

STUPID
I just want to second reader "MOST DISGUSTED"'s letter. If anyone has the simplest grasp of life, has the merest ability to comprehend the complex philosophy we live by, they would realize instantly why we have wars, why we have sickness and disease. They would realize in a sentence like "MOST DISGUSTED," that women are stupid! DISGUSTED BOY

STUPID
In answer to the vital argument "MOST DISGUSTED"'s letter has touched off, I think the truth of the matter is men and women are stupid! DISGUSTED THING

KILL
I think that the solution to our problems is to kill all the Democrats. DISGUSTED REPUBLICAN

KILL
I think the solution to our problems is to kill all the Republicans. DISGUSTED DEMOCRAT

KILL
I think the solution to our problems is to kill everybody. PLAIN DISGUSTED.

...more feature... then... movie ads! These movie ads certainly do untold damage to grown-ups!

requited, what is your answer?
ANSWER: Yes.

DEAR MISS UNREQUIT-ED: I am going out who sometimes I think don't love me. He don't have a job, and once we had a date and I gave him my pay-check to take us out and when he took me home I asked him for the change and he told me to leave him alone or he'd never take me out again. Next time we had a date, I gave him my car for us to take a ride in. When he took me home, I asked for the car and he told me to leave him alone or he'd never take me for a ride again. Next time we had a date, he was with another girl. When he asked him to take me home. He told me to leave him alone or he'd get me in trouble. What I want to know is, can he get me in trouble?—Z.X.
ANSWER: Maybe.

...another man who ... out to be the first man worked for. When I met the first man, it was love at first sight, and since he had divorced the second woman, he thought everything was all right till the first woman showed up. Now everything is in a furshlugginer mess and I am wondering if you have any opinion on all this. Miss Un-

★★★★★ WHAT'S
UP-STARS

YOUR HOROSCOPE
by Steller Smurdley
Today—the stars predict many important events, so take careful note. First of all, it seems that the morning will start very early, and later on in the day you will find your-self in the afternoon. Still later on, in the late afternoon, it will get very dark and you will be very sleepy. Our advice would be for you to go to bed. During the

Also, try to eat and breathe and most of all, stay alive.

Gemini—Today to all Geminis who have birthdays, all we have to say to you is, Jiminy, all Gemini, happy birthday! For all Gemini, nomatter homini, we predict that today your future lies ahead of you although your past is behind.

★★★★★
LATE LATE
LATE LATE

4,000 Pages

DAILY ✤ POOP

PICTURE NEWSPAPER...PLENTY PICTURES

Copr. 1954 Poop Syndicate Co. Inc.

Someday, October, 1954★

4¢ IN CITY LIMITS 4¢ OUTSIDE CITY LIMITS 5¢ COUNTRY LIMITS 6¢ OUTSIDE EARTH LIMITS

4¢ A POUND

10 PAGES BLOODY FIGHT PICS

...finally—the back page which is a page which is a shame to civilization sometimes!

Full Nauseating Story on Page 980

Messiest Fight Ever

Here are the Daily Poop's exclusive fight pics of the Kid Smadoodley—Punchy Melvin bout. The Poop has spared no expense to give you complete photo coverage of best and bloodiest parts of fight blows, taken from many different angles. Candid shot on left [←] catches face of Punchy Melvin as it contorts from Smadoodley's left to the head. Next candid shot [→] catches Kid's contorted face pressed unbelievably flat for an instant by Punchy's glove. Below, left [↙] Punchy's face contorted . ear is where eye should be. Last shot [←] Kid's whole face is in space eyebrows should be.

(POOP foto by Jack POTRZEBIE)

(POOP foto by Jack Davis)

(POOP foto by Jack Davis)

Man Fined For Bashing Son

This photo [→] shows grown-up accused of severely spanking youthful son [→]. Grown-up told reporters how while reading newspaper today, he noticed youth looking at evil reading matter. Suddenly, grown-up's mind felt so strangely corrupted, he jumped up and spanked youth [→]. Youth [→] points [→] to wrench [←] grownup [↑] used to [↓] spank.

WELL, YOUTH...THAT'S WHAT THEY'RE READING! THAT'S WHAT MONEY-HUNGRY PUBLISHERS ARE FEEDING TO OUR OWN GROWN-UPS!... YOU CAN ACT!...FORM CLUBS, ORGANIZATIONS!...SEE TO IT THAT OUR GROWN-UPS BUY CLEAN WHOLESOME READING MATTER! SEE TO IT THAT OUR GROWN-UPS ARE NOT CORRUPTED BY NEWSPAPERS!

Do you hear people snickering faintly behind your back as you ride to school or work? Examine the situation! Is the comic book you are reading one of the kind with the loud, garish covers? No wonder people laugh! Do you want to look like an idiot reading comic books all your life?

. . . If you don't, then listen to this! MAD comic book has a new cover design that makes it look like high-class literature! Buy the latest issue of MAD, then you can look like an idiot reading high-class literature! Buy MAD . . . it's milder . . . much milder.

42

You have no doubt noticed how in certain comic-books, the publishers stick in "seals"—seals of "approval" which they award themselves. Since we want to get along with everybody too, and make money, we also are sticking in a "seal"—the very first seal, we might add, of "disapproval"—for this our story about Pulaski Street's typical teen-ager . . . .

Starchie

· DISAPPROVED · READING

ANOTHER MAD MIND WARPER

45

46

48

50

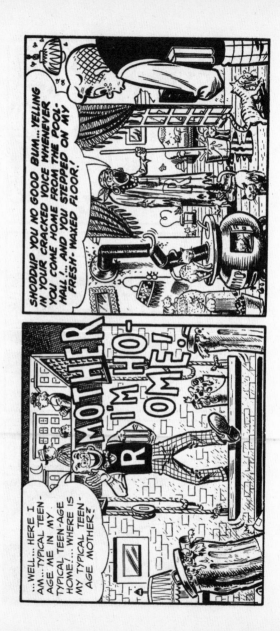

59

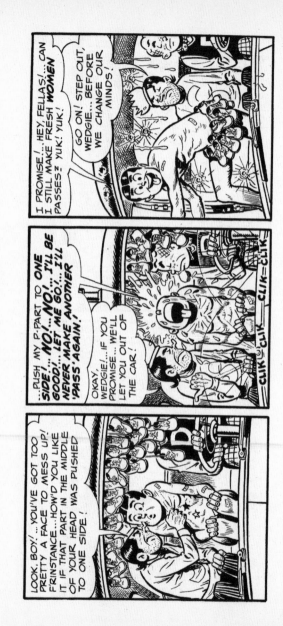

62

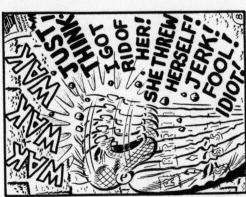

WAAAA! JUST THINK! I GOT RID OF HER! SHE THREW HERSELF! JERK! FOOL! IDIOT!

I THINK OF OLD HIGH SCHOOL ADVENTURES...HOW BIDDY USED TO THROW HERSELF AT ME AND I WOULD TRY TO GET RID OF HER... AS I THINK OF THESE NOSTALGIC MEMORIES...I AM DEEPLY MOVED AND THERE IS ONLY ONE THING I CAN DO AND THAT ONE THING IS...

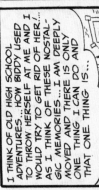

...AND NOW, MY TYPICAL TEEN-AGE DAYS ARE PASSED, AND I HAVE BUT A FEW SCRAPS HERE TO REMIND ME OF DAYS GONE BY!...A FEW DUSTY PHOTOGRAPHS OF SALONICA AND BIDDY...THE BOW-TIE, SWEATER AND CHECKED PANTS I WORE (WHICH I AM STILL WEARING)! ...AND AS I LOOK AT THE YELLOWING PHOTOGRAPHS...THE PICTURES OF MY FRIENDS...OF BIDDY...

Well . . . Here we go with another miserable story! Gather 'round, you readers! . . . Pull up your toadstools and wet rocks and get nice and cozy . . . that's right, settle down where it's nice and dank and we'll tell you a story we call . . . .

FLESH GARDEN!

WHAT KIND OF A CREATURE LIES BEHIND THAT BLOOD-STAINED OAKEN DOOR? COULD IT BE WORSE THAN THE SLIME-OOZING, KNIFE-TOOTHED *ZORK*?

ULP!...THE DOOR IS SLOWLY OPENING! COULD IT BE ANY WORSE THAN THE HAIRY, MANY-CLAWED *ZORCHTON*?

GULP!...THERE'S SOMETHING STANDING THERE! COULD IT BE ANY WORSE THAN THE PALPITATING, LIMB-RIPPING, *ZILCHTRON*?

GASP! I CAN SEE IT NOW...WORSE THAN THE *ZORK*...MORE TERRIBLE THAN THE *ZORCHTON*...MORE HORRIBLE THAN THE *ZILCHTRON*... IT'S...IT'S...IT'S...

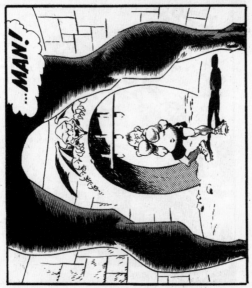

BEWARE OF IMITATIONS!
NO CREDIT
KANDY
MAGAZINES
ALL
MID
MOD
MED
MOOD
MORD
MIRD
MARD
MURD
MAHD
MHAD
MHAHD
MADD
MADDD
MMAD
MAAAD
MADMAD
MAD
MAD
MUD
MDD
SHMAD
ADMAY
MAYAD
MYAD
MAYD
MD
M
MZD
MQD
MKD
MAD

BEWARE OF IMITATIONS!... THERE ARE MANY IMITATORS OF *MAD* WHO WOULD HAVE YOU BELIEVE THAT THEIR PRODUCT IS SUPERIOR TO MAD!... HOWEVER, ONLY *MAD* USES YOUNG, TENDER PAGES THAT ARE SEASONED IN OUR WARE-HOUSE!... DON'T TAKE OUR WORD FOR IT!... MAKE THIS SIMPLE TASTE-TEST!

First...shred up an issue of *MAD* magazine! Put it in your mouth! Chew it a while and then swallow it... Notice how fresh the ink tastes... how it tickles your tummy?

CHOMP
CHOMP!

Then...take any other magazine and eat it!...Horrible, isn't it! Notice how sick you feel! Notice how your heart is slowing up... and soon it will stop completely!

OOP

Make the taste-test yourself! Make the taste-test and you will see why leading doctors say that more people eat *MAD* than any other comic magazines!

REMEMBER!... MAD! IS MILDER... MUCH MILDER!

The story you are about to hear is false! . . . Only the names have been changed to protect the publishers! And now MAD, the comic that is highest in quality . . . lowest in nicotine, with no irritation to nose, throat or sinuses . . . MAD presents . . .

DRAGGED NET!

94

AT 9:30, WE WENT ON STAKE-OUT! WHEN ONE IS ON STAKE-OUT, ONE MUSTN'T LET ANYTHING DISTRACT ONE!

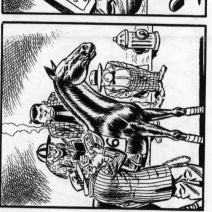

AT FIRST WHEN THE CHIEF SENT US ON STAKE-OUT... WE RAN TO A RES-TAURANT... WE THOUGHT HE MEANT STEAK-OUT!

...NOW WE'RE ON STAKE-OUT... SPECIAL ASSIGNMENT... AND ONE MUSTN'T LET *ANY-THING* DISTRACT ONE WHILE ON STAKE-OUT...

...WELL!... *MOST* ANYTHING!

AT 9:30, WE WENT BACK TO OUR STAKE-OUT... OUR ASSIGNMENT, WATCHING AND WAITING AT THIS CORNER!

...A LITTLE LATER, AT 9:30, THE HAIL WAS REPLACED BY SNOW... BUT WE WERE ON STAKE-OUT...

...AND WHEN ONE IS ON STAKE-OUT, ONE MUST NOT...ABSOLUTELY MUST NOT LEAVE ONE'S POST UNDER ANY CIRCUMSTANCES!

...WELL! **MOST** ANY CIRCUMSTANCES!

108

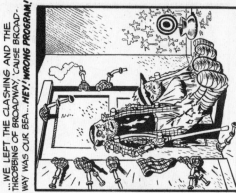

AT 9:30, WE LEFT OUR STAKE-OUT! WE LEFT OUR STAKE-OUT BECAUSE WE HAD GOTTEN WHAT WE WAITED FOR!

...WE HAD GOTTEN WHAT OUR CHIEF HAD SENT US FOR AND SO WE LEFT THE NEON ILLUMINATED STREETS...

...WE LEFT THE CLASHING AND THE THROBBING OF BROADWAY, 'CAUSE BROADWAY WAS OUR BEA... *HEY! WRONG PROGRAM!*

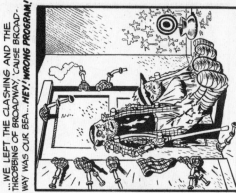

BEWARE OF IMITATIONS!... MANY OF OUR COMPETITORS ARE PUTTING OUT MAGAZINES THAT ARE IMITATIONS...FILTHY UN-AMERICAN SWIPES OF *MAD* MAGAZINE...IF YOU WANT TO AVOID IMITATIONS...MAKE THIS SIMPLE TEST...

First...roll up a *MAD* magazine! Light it! Take a couple puffs! ...Notice how slowly the paper burns!... Notice how gently it sets your head on fire!

...Now take any other magazine and light it. Notice the oily brown poisonous colony of the smoke... the hotness of the melted staples on your tongue!

...Yes...once you make this test, we guarantee you will never smoke an imitation magazine again...You will never do *nuttin'* ever again!

REMEMBER!...MAD IS MILDER...*MUCH MILDER!*

We have a scene from a Television show that began in April and that by now every man, woman and child in the U.S.A. should be familiar with! Although this show was originally programmed for two weeks . . . it ran a lot longer and for a while it looked like it'd be sustaining. . . .

Now, if you even glanced at it you were no doubt struck by the monotony of this show! . . . The lack of plot . . . the repetitious dialogue . . . the dull, uninteresting scenery with the same camera angles, again and again! . . . We of MAD respectfully suggest that the approach to this show was all wrong . . . and with an eye toward constructive criticism we offer on the following pages our suggestion as to how it should have been done.

First of all . . . . who wants to listen to a program called "The Senate Subcommittee Hearings on the Army Investigations"? . . . The whole thing needed a snappier title . . . like for instance, "Truth or Cohnsequences," . . . "Break the Rank'" . . . or . . . .

WHAT'S MY SHINE!

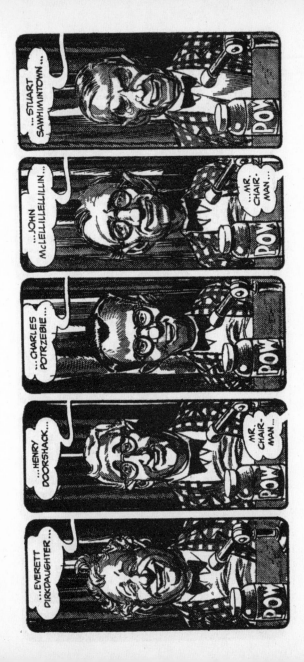

122

123

HERE IS THE ORIGINAL PHOTOGRAPH AS IT LOOKED BEFORE IT WAS DOCTORED! YOU WILL NOTICE THAT THE 'WARBONNET' IS A TURKEY SITTING ON A FENCE BEHIND EVEN STEVEN!... YOU WILL NOTICE THE 'WAR-PAINT' IS HOUSE-PAINT EVEN STEVEN WAS SPATTERED WITH WHILE PAINTING HOUSE WITH 'TOMAHAWK' WHICH IS IN REALITY A PAINT-ROLLER!

WHICH ALL GOES TO PROVE I AM NOT AND NEVER HAVE BEEN A RED-SKIN!

NOW 'EVEN'... NO NEED TO RAISE YOUR VOICE AND GET ANGRY! I REALIZE YOU'RE NOT REALLY A REDSKIN BUT MERELY A DUPE OF THE REDSKINS! I'M NOT MAD AND I'M WILLING TO SETTLE THIS ALL VERY QUICKLY IN THE HONEST, STRAIGHTFORWARD MANNER THAT IS THE INTELLIGENT WAY TO DISCUSS DIFFERENCES OF OPINION AND THAT SIMPLE MANNER IS...

...THAT SIMPLE MANNER IS...

133

ARMSTRONGER TIRE

Knock-Down Punch Socko For Skids!

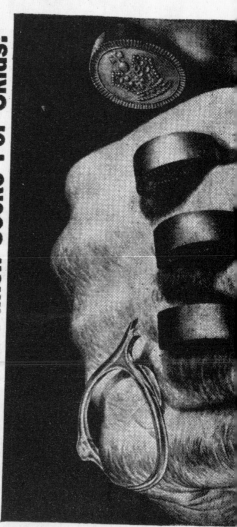

Armstronger Patented Safety Discs Protect You As No Other Tubeless Tire Can!

Eller

Photos on the left demonstrate why Armstronger Tires give you the greatest skid protection in tire history. And remember, skids are the *major* cause of accidents and lost purposes.

So today—get the world's only tire with Patented Safety Discs. They can save you plenty accidents in a fist fight. And if the discs alone don't work . . . try hitting with the whole tire.

Just like the edges of your fist, tread ribs of ordinary tires tend to compress into a smooth and slippery surface under pressure. Under pressure the tread loses its vital grip . . . *and you skid!*

With Armstronger tires, Patented Safety Discs *keep gripping edges apart!* No longer do you skid as you deftly pluck Patented Safety Discs from Armstronger tire and insert them in your fist.

ARMSTRONGER

Rhino-ceris

Tireless Tubas

Only Armstronger gives this LIFETIME UNCONDITIONAL GUARANTEE guaranteed unconditionally you *will* live your whole lifetime or your money back!

Armstronger's tire gives you straight line stop with slow and gentle musical hissing sound instead of usual ugly explosion punctured tire makes.

POETRY DEPT.: THERE IS A FAMOUS POEM WHOSE NAME IS USED NO MORE! . . . YOU'VE HEARD OF IT BY TITLE IT REALLY NEVER WORE (. . . AND IF YOU HAVEN'T HEARD . . . WELL, KID, YOU JUST DON'T KNOW THE SCORE!) . . . AS TIME HAS PASSED, THE NEWER NAME HAS SUBSTITUTED FOR . . . *THE FACE UPON THE BARROOM FLOOR FOR . . .*

THE FACE UPON THE FLOOR!

BY H. ANTOINE D'ARCY

"Where did it come from?" someone said: "The wind
    has blown it in."
"What does it want?" another cried. "Some whisky,
    rum or gin?"

"Here, Toby, seek him, if your stomach's equal
    to the work —
I wouldn't touch him with a fork, he's filthy as a
    Turk."

This badinage the poor wretch took with stoical good grace;
In fact, he smiled as though he thought he'd struck the proper place.[a]

"Come, boys, I know there's kindly hearts among so good a crowd—
To be in such good company would make a deacon proud.

"Give me a drink—that's what I want—I'm out of funds, you know; When I had cash to treat the gang, this hand was never slow.

"What? You laugh as though you thought this pocket never held a sou; I once was fixed as well, my boys, as anyone of you.

"There, thanks; that's braced me nicely; God bless you 'Give you a song? No, I can't do that, my singing
one and all;   days are past;
Next time I pass this good saloon, I'll make   My voice is cracked, my throat's worn out, and my
another call.   lungs are going fast.

"Say: Give me another whisky, and I'll tell
    what I'll do —
I'll tell you a funny story, and a fact, I promise
    too.

"That I was ever a decent man not one of you
    would think;
But I was, some four or five years back. Say, give
    me another drink.

"Fill her up, Joe, I want to put some life into my frame—
Such little drinks, to a bum like me, are miserably tame;
"Five fingers—there, that's the scheme—and corking whisky, too.
Well, here's luck, boys; and, landlord, my best regards to you."

"You've treated me pretty kindly, and I'd like to tell you how
I came to be the dirty sot you see before you now.

"As I told you, once I was a man, with muscle,
frame and health,
And, but for a blunder, ought to have made
considerable wealth.

"I was a painter – not one that daubed on bricks and wood
But an artist, and, for my age, was rated pretty good.

"I worked hard, at my canvas and was bidding fair to rise,
For gradually I saw the star of fame before my eyes.

"I made a picture, perhaps you've seen, 'tis called "And then I met a woman — now comes the
the 'Chase of Fame,'   funny part—
It brought me fifteen hundred pounds and   With eyes that petrified my brain, and sunk
added to my name.   into my heart.

"Why don't you laugh? 'Tis funny that the vagabond
you see
Could ever love a woman and expect her love
for me; –

"But 'twas so, and for a month or two, her
smiles were freely given,
And when her loving lips touched mine it
carried me to heaven.

"Did ever you see a woman for whom your soul
you'd give
With a form like Milo Venus, too beautiful to
live;

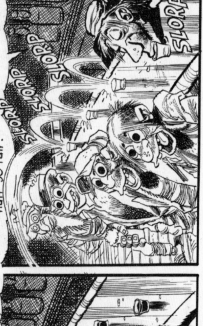

"With eyes that would beat the Koh-i-noor, and
a wealth of chestnut hair?
If so, 'twas she, for there never was another
half so fair.

"I was working on a portrait, one afternoon in May,
Of a fair-haired boy, a friend of mine, who lived across the way.

"And Madeline admired it, and much to my surprise,
Said that she'd like to know the man that had such dreamy eyes.

"It didn't take long to know him, and before the month had flown
My friend had stolen my darling, and I was left alone;
And, ere a year of misery had passed above my head,
The jewel I had treasured so had tarnished, and was dead.

"Why, what's the matter, friend? There's a teardrop in your eye;
Come, laugh like me; 'tis only babes and women that should cry.

"That's why I took to drink, boys. Why, I never saw you smile,
I thought you'd be amused, and laughing all the while.

152

"Say, boys, if you give me just another whisky,
I'll be glad,
And I'll draw right here a picture of the face
that drove me mad."

"Give me that piece of chalk with which you
mark the baseball score —
You shall see the lovely Madeline upon the
barroom floor."

Another drink, and with the chalk in hand, the vagabond began
To sketch a face that well might buy the soul of any man.

Then, as he placed another lock upon the shapely head,
With fearful shriek, he leaped and fell across the picture— dead.

"My beer is Potgold
—the Dry beer!"

says HESTER SHVESTER
MISS POTGOLD 1954

Beer as beer should taste!

Yes...Potgold beer is refreshing — never filling! Potgold's extra dryness let's you taste the clean, clear, beer flavor. Potgold beer is beer as beer should taste! Yes sir, we guarantee Potgold tastes *just like beer!*

Potgold
EXTRA DRY

REGULAR   KING-SIZE

155

Say . . . bet you old-timers will like this one. Remember way back when this comic strip started? You were a lot younger then. Men were wearing straw hats. Women's fashions were ridiculous. Fort Sumter was being fired upon. Remember? Enough reminiscing and on to our story . . .

159

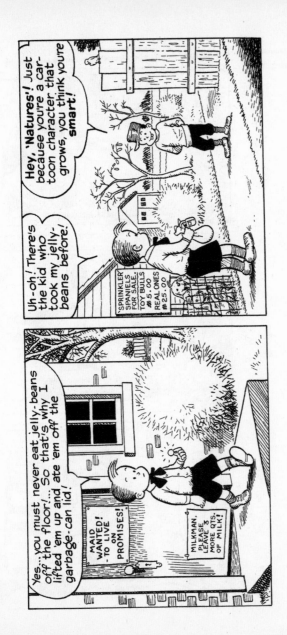

163

...I'll bet that veeblefetzers are cracking every day all over town!... Why don't we start a cracked veeblefetzer fixing company... Willit and Booble... cracked veeblefetzers fixers!
...I'll shake on that!
Note to readers: Naturally, there is no such thing as a veeblefetzer! This grotesque designation is used merely to disguise our real operation which is such a good idea that we want to protect the idea from being stolen by any unscrupulous operators... mainly you readers!
DRIVE SLOW. HELP KEEP OUR STREETS CLEAN!!!

Gosh!... We've got a shed set up and we're really in business! Won't Nin be surprised when I tell her how business has **doubled** since I started out today? Started out with **one** cracked veeblefetzer and we now have **two**!
WILLIT & BOOBLE
SCRABBLE BOARDS REPAIRED.

172

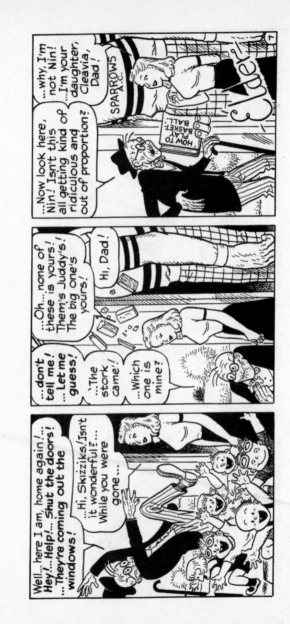

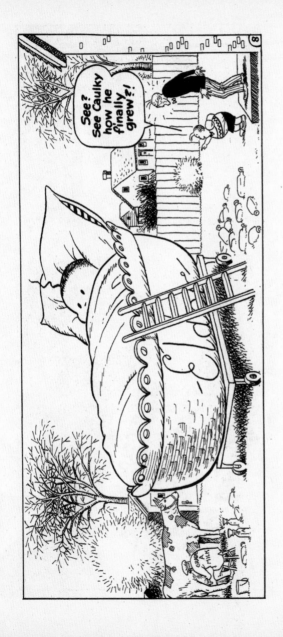

"My beer ish
Potgold
zha Dry beer."
—says HESTER SHVESTER
MISS POTGOLD 1954

182

And now, let us tell a story of yesteryear, when law and order rode the plains on a white stallion behind a Black Mask! . . . Look! Here he comes! A fiery horse with the speed of light . . . a cloud of dust and a hearty HIYO GOLDEN! It's the . . . .

LONE STRANGER!

184

THE MEN WHO MAKE MAD

HARVEY KURTZMAN, beagle editor, is married and has two bagles (baby beagles). Drawing from his experience in composing MAD . . . seeing how he's creating laughter, happiness, making living easier in this troubled world, Kurtzman now sees what his ideals, what his purpose, his goal should be. Kurtzman now understands what is the most precious thing in life. These ideals, this purpose, this goal, this precious thing in life is . . . mainly . . . money.

BILL ELDER is a complete idiot. He is kept locked in a steel cage in Englewood, N. J., where once a month his hairy, claw-like hand is seen to emerge through a trap in the door with a set of drawings. Then, clutching a slab of raw beef (Elder gets paid in raw beef), the hand withdraws into the darkness, not to be seen again until the next month.

JACK DAVIS is a colorful character from the deep South. On a clear summer day, Jack can be seen charging from the elevator, shrieking the rebel yell down the hall to the comic-book office, where he demolishes the door pane with his percussion rifle, spears his pay check with his needle bayonet, and dashes away to buy Confederate money.

WALLACE WOOD, as well as being a fine comic cartoonist, is one of the leading science-fiction cartoonists in the U. S. One is amazed . . . often puzzled . . . at the authentic quality and detail of Wood's drawings of machines from outer space. And even more baffling is the third eye one occasionally sees, concealed as it is in a furrow of Wood's forehead.

From ibooks—

The *MAD* Reader
MAD Strikes Back!
Inside *MAD*
Utterly *MAD*
The Brothers *MAD*